The Chipmunk Who Wanted to Be a Bear

Written by Valerie Harmon
Concept & Illustrations by Carol Stevens

For information regarding purchases, please contact:
Wantstobe.com

ISBN-13: 978-1500281557

Manufactured in the United States of America

Dedications

To Cory, who is willing to put aside his fears and try something difficult (as a toddler he also used to store food in his cheeks just like Chipmunk).—Carol Stevens

To Solomon, who knows all about conquering fears.—Valerie Harmon

Author's Note

I grew up in a forest, so this story reminded me of my childhood. However, I never met a grizzly bear, although I have fed bread to chipmunks. They are very cute! I didn't mention this in the story, but like bears, chipmunks hibernate in winter. While bears sleep deeply the whole winter and live off their fat, chipmunks actually wake up periodically to snack on their stored seeds and nuts. I know many of you love science— so I want to be sure and give you the right facts.

May you set goals and work hard to reach them too,

—Valerie Harmon

High up a mountain, inside a hole of a tall fir tree, lived a chipmunk. It may sound scary to live in a tree-top, but this chipmunk wasn't scared of his home—he was scared to leave it! Every time he ventured out to get food or water, his heart raced and his paws trembled.

As Chipmunk looked down from his tree he saw a grizzly bear fishing in the river. The massive bear didn't look scared of anything as he scooped up a fish for his dinner. Suddenly, Chipmunk had an idea.

Chipmunk dropped an acorn on the grizzly bear's nose. Startled, the bear looked up.

"H-h-hello Bear," Chipmunk stuttered. "I'm s-s-scared of everything. If I were a b-b-bear, then maybe I wouldn't be so af-f-fraid all the time. C-c-could you help me become a b-b-bear?"

Bear had just eaten a big meal, so he didn't mind chatting with the chipmunk. Plus, he wanted to help the poor frightened creature. "Do you believe *anything* is possible?" he asked. Chipmunk nodded.

"Well then," Bear rumbled kindly, "bears fish for their dinner, maybe you should learn to fish. Try it for a week." He lumbered off as Chipmunk clutched a branch and tried to catch his breath. He had done it! He'd spoken to the huge bear and lived. Now he just had to learn to catch fish and he could become a brave bear too!

Chipmunk reviewed his plan for fishing and then began. He snuck down his tree and paused under a large root. Looking from side to side, up and around, he couldn't smell or hear anything that might want to eat him. Whew! He dashed into the river and stood still, waiting for the waves to disappear—and for his heart to calm down. Suddenly, he saw movement underwater. In an instant, he scooped up TWO minnows with his front paws. He stuffed the minnows into his cheeks to store like acorns. But unlike acorns, they wriggled to get free! It tickled so much that Chipmunk couldn't hold them so he spit them out.

He stood in the water, savoring the moment. On his first try, he had fished and caught! This was fabulous! This was momentous! This was amazing! Chipmunk did a little dance.

Fishing was so much fun that he spent the whole day catching and releasing minnows. As Chipmunk watched the last one swim away, he decided that tomorrow he would be ready for bigger fish.

The next day, Chipmunk jumped onto a rock in the middle of the river. He waited, and waited, and waited. The sun baked his fur. The water reflected the sunshine. The rock felt hot and uncomfortable. But he forced himself to be patient. Finally glimpsing movement underwater, he leaped with his outstretched paws, ready to catch the trout. But the trout caught him instead.

"Riding a trout was the scariest feeling ever," thought Chipmunk as he ran all the way home and crawled into his bed. It took several days for Chipmunk to shake off his fear and remember how excited he had felt catching those minnows. He hated feeling frightened, and the bear had spoken so kindly to him. He took a deep breath, crept out of his cozy home, and found Bear in a meadow.

"I c-c-caught two minnows, and then a t-t-trout caught me," explained Chipmunk, trembling as Bear huffed a laugh. "But I'm still not a bear, w-w-what can I d-d-do?"

"You are braver than you think," Bear responded, as he walked away. "But maybe you could learn to talk like a bear."

"How do bears talk?" Chipmunk asked himself. "Does Bear want me to learn to growl and roar?"

"Rawrrr," Chipmunk said, his growl sounding like a squeaking mouse. He shook his head, took a deep breath, deepened his voice and pushed it louder, "Rawrrr." That was better.

He saw a butterfly resting on a leaf. He crept behind it, and roared, "Rawrrrr!" The butterfly flew away and Chipmunk giggled to himself. He had roared!

Puffed with success, Chipmunk looked for another creature to growl at. He saw a raccoon. Creeping among the ferns, he jumped in front of the raccoon and roared, "Rawrrr!"

The raccoon froze. Then he covered his mouth and laughed. And laughed. And laughed.

Chipmunk slunk home, with his tail dragging and his shoulders drooping. But by the next day, the humiliating feeling had disappeared, and Chipmunk kept roaring to himself and remembering the startled butterfly. Did he want to be a bear? Yes! So he left his comfortable home and looked for Bear.

He found Bear napping by a log. "Rawrrr!" Chipmunk exclaimed. Bear opened one eye. "So you know how to roar now?"

"Yes! But I'm still not a bear!"

"Well," Bear began, with a big yawn, "Perhaps you should sleep more. Bears hibernate all winter." As Bear closed his eyes, Chipmunk took the hint and left. He headed straight to bed, even though it was midday. It felt very odd to Chipmunk. He was not used to naps.

It had been a busy day, but Chipmunk couldn't make his mind rest. He scrunched himself into his soft bedding. He relaxed his paws. He closed his eyes. But he kept remembering his feeling of triumph when he caught the minnows or when the butterfly flew away at his roar. And then he would feel like jumping up and squeaking a cheer. Finally he drifted off to sleep, counting flying minnows with butterfly wings.

When he awoke, it was the middle of the night. Outside his tree house, everything was dark. But it wasn't silent. He heard the eerie hoot of an owl and the chirping of crickets. Sleep was impossible with all these noises of the night. Feeling braver than usual, Chipmunk poked his head out and growled, "Rawrr! Please be quiet." When the crickets stopped chirping, he thought maybe he was becoming a bear after all. After a week of trying...

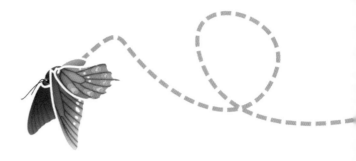

Finally, on the last day...

At the last hour...

At the last minute...

Ka-Poof!

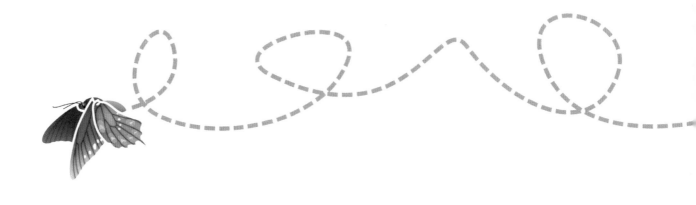

Chipmunk transformed into something greater. He became Chizzly! He kept his chipmunk lines and long tail, but he was as big as a grizzly bear. He opened his mouth and roared, listening to it echo off the mountains.

Sometimes Chizzly would tell jokes to the raccoons, who would always laugh at his joke, but never laugh at him. But most of all...

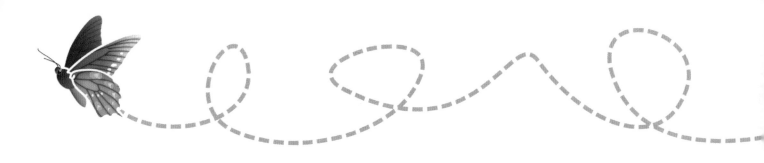

...**C**hizzly loved to go fishing with his pal Bear.

34

About the Author and Illustrator

Valerie Harmon

Valerie Harmon graduated with a BA in English and teaches writing and Shakespeare. At the end of the school year she directs a Shakespeare play that her students perform. She's a voracious reader, a free-lance editor, blogger and Mom to six children. She lives in the Western United States with her children, husband, and more books than bookshelves.

Carol Stevens

Carol Stevens graduated with a BFA in Illustration and works as a graphic designer and free-lance illustrator. She and her husband have five children. Her family has gotten a lot smaller these past few years, but she has all the aging pets the children have left behind. She lives in the Western United States.

When her youngest was born (ten years after her fourth child) she needed some new material for bedtime storytelling. The idea for this book came from that busy time as a Mom with teenagers and a toddler. Each night her son would pick two different animals and Carol had to come up with three new challenges to keep it interesting. Her son enjoyed the stories so much, and they were so funny, that she decided this concept should be her first picture book series. She highly recommends that you do this story time activity with your children!

More Titles at Wantstobe.com

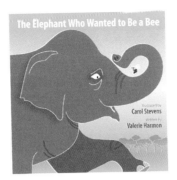

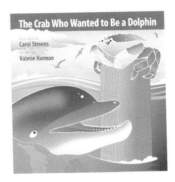

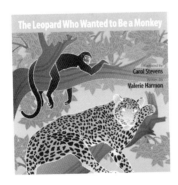

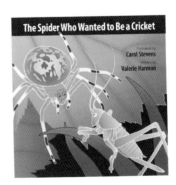

Want to hear Bear roar or help Chipmunk catch a fish? Check out the app version for iPad, complete with sound effects, animations, and narration. Go to our website for information on our other print publications, apps and ebooks.

Made in the USA
San Bernardino, CA
26 August 2014